The Mightiest Heart

By LYNN CULLEN

Illustrated by LAUREL LONG

Dial Books for Young Readers

New York

Published by Dial Books for Young Readers
A member of Penguin Putnam Inc.
375 Hudson Street
New York, New York 10014

Designed by Nancy R. Leo
Printed in Hong Kong on acid-free paper
First Edition
3 5 7 9 10 8 6 4 2

Library of Congress Cataloging in Publication Data
Cullen, Lynn.
The mightiest heart/by Lynn Cullen; illustrated by Laurel Long.—1st ed.
p.   cm.
Summary: Based on a Welsh legend about Prince Llywelyn and his loyal dog,
Gelert, who is wrongly banished when the prince believes that
the dog has attacked his son.
ISBN 0-8037-2292-3 (trade).—ISBN 0-8037-2293-1 (lib. bdg.)
[1. Folklore—Wales.] I. Long, Laurel, ill. II. Title.
PZ8.1.C894Mi 1998   398.2—DC21   97-26676   CIP   AC

The art for this book was created using oil paints on
watercolor paper primed with gesso.

rince Llywelyn was the luckiest lad in Wales. He lived in a tall stone castle in the mountains of Snowdonia. He had a hawk that soared high from his glove. He had strong ponies to ride; servants to grant his every wish; a table set with jellied eel and roast peacock. But what made Llywelyn truly lucky was his dog, Gelert.

From his earliest days as a pup, Gelert's only desire was to be at Llywelyn's side. If Llywelyn chased hares in the meadow, Gelert was there. If Llywelyn climbed trees in the wood, Gelert was there. If Llywelyn counted the stars in the sky, Gelert was beside him.

For Betsy, Bobby, and Nancy—L.C.
For Stephen, Shea, and Ronny—L.L.

Never did Gelert leave Llywelyn. Not when Llywelyn jumped from stone to mossy stone in the brook–and the stones did not fit four paws.

Not when Llywelyn raced across meadows dotted with sheep and through fields being turned–and Gelert did not know to hide from the shepherds and plowmen.

Not when Llywelyn dashed across the drawbridge as it closed–and Gelert was two steps behind.

And especially not when shadows crept from the wood, nor when wolves howled from the hilltop.

But as Llywelyn grew, there was less time for chasing hares in the meadow, climbing trees in the wood, and counting the stars in the sky. Befitting a prince who would become a leader of men, Llywelyn learned the art of war. He practiced how to strike with his sword and aim his lance, and he mastered riding a charging warhorse. Whole days would go by with nothing except a hurried pat to Gelert's head from Llywelyn. But that was enough for Gelert.

The day came when Llywelyn asked a king's daughter for her hand in marriage. The wedding was a grand affair, and all of Snowdonia feasted in the castle's Great Hall. Gelert, a rose tucked under his collar, remained at his master's side, little noticed but very proud.

Because Llywelyn loved the new princess, Gelert loved her too. She, however, did not fancy Gelert. "He makes my gown stink of hound," she complained to Llywelyn. The prince had no choice but to banish the dog from their chamber. Gelert then waited for his master by the bedchamber door.

In time the princess bore a son, and all of Wales rejoiced. Llywelyn dreamed of the days when he and his son would chase hares in the meadow, climb trees in the wood, and count stars in the sky.

Now Gelert's greatest desire was to lick the infant's wrinkled red face. But the princess declared, "I trust him not." So Gelert was banished from the nursery. He found a new post in the courtyard, where he patiently waited for Llywelyn's call.

One day, after a council in the Great Hall with his lords,
Llywelyn bounded into the nursery, eager to see his baby son after
troubling talk of war.

"Dafydd!" he called joyously.

But when he looked into his son's cradle, he found it empty and
marked with blood.

"Dafyyd!" he called again, this time in horror.

A whimper came from the corner. Llywelyn whirled around
to find Gelert, his jaws red with blood.

When he awoke, his face was wet. A thin old dog stood over him, licking his cheek. On the other side of the brook a wolf lay dead.

Llywelyn struggled to a sit. "Gelert?"

The dog, bleeding from a fresh wound, licked Llywelyn once more. The prince threw his arms around the dog. "Gelert!" He rested his face against the dog's withered side. And the last sound he heard before darkness closed in again was the steady beating of his old friend's heart.

When Llywelyn awoke a second time, stars shone through the treetops, too numerous to count. But Gelert was gone.

Weak from his wounds, Llywelyn piled stone upon mossy stone, not stopping though his hands grew raw and his feet numb. At last a mound as high as Llywelyn himself stood in the place where Gelert had appeared. When Llywelyn turned for home, he little noticed the hares springing through the meadow.

With an anguished roar, Llywelyn attacked Gelert. "Murderer!" He raised his sword over the cowering dog, ready to strike, when a cry came from beneath the cradle.

Llywelyn dropped to his knees and lifted the bedclothes. There was Dafydd, blinking in the light.

Llywelyn rushed the babe to the window, but when he examined his son, he found not a scratch. His gaze fell on a trail of blood on the windowsill. Only then did he look below and see the wolf lying in the snow, its throat stained with blood.

"Gelert!" Llywelyn whispered. But when he turned around, the dog was gone.

Llywelyn searched for
Gelert high and low, even as one
season passed into the next.
Careworn and weary, Llywelyn
kept up his hunt. But Gelert
could not be found.

One day Llywelyn was riding
alone through the wood in the
valley, his troubles heavy on his
mind. War hung like a black
cloud over Wales, and many of
his lords had turned against him.
The princess offered him little
solace, for her heart had grown
cold. He was deep in thought,
his horse splashing through the
very brook where Llywelyn
once played, when the wolf
attacked. Llywelyn tumbled to
the bank, and all went black.

Seasons passed, and though war savaged Llywelyn's land, plowmen still turned the fields and shepherds tended their sheep. Then one day young Dafydd dashed into the Great Hall, where his father sat staring into the fire.

"Father, look! Can I have him?"

Llywelyn bolted upright as if an arrow had pierced his heart.
The pup was the very image of Gelert.

"Can I keep him, sir?" Dafydd begged. "I found him in the
wood."

"Which wood?"

"The wood in the valley, sir. By the brook, by that pile of
stones. He was alone."

Shyly the pup licked Llywelyn's hand.

Llywelyn fought to control his pounding heart. At last he said,
"You may keep him on one condition."

"Yes, sir! Anything!"

"That you never let him go."

Dafydd laughed. "Let him go? Why would I?"

A log broke in the fire, crashing with a swirl of sparks. The pup
squirmed in Dafydd's arms.

"Go, Son," said Llywelyn. "Treat him well. And mind you this—the mightiest heart can come in the humblest vessel."

"Of course, sir," said the boy, looking puzzled. Then he buried his nose in the pup's soft fur, and brightened. "Now I shall be the luckiest lad in Wales!"

Llywelyn, staring into the sizzling fire whispered back, "That you shall be, my son. That you shall be."

Author's Note

There truly is a Snowdonia. It's a place in Wales of tree-covered mountains, where dogs herd sheep across sloping meadows, gray stone houses huddle against the hillsides, and brooks—dark with mossy stones—wind their way through the shadows of valleys. If fairies exist, they live here.

There truly was a Prince Llywelyn. He lived from the late-twelfth century to the mid-thirteenth century, and led the Welsh people in a move for independence from England. He truly did marry the daughter of a king—Joan, the daughter of King John of England. However, this did not stop him from fighting the king for freedom. And Llywelyn did indeed pay dearly for his years of battle. Weary of war and broken-hearted after the discovery of his wife's unfaithfulness, he became a monk, living out his last two years in silence.

In the mountains of Snowdonia there is an actual grave marking the resting place of Prince Llywelyn's loyal wolfhound, Gelert. Gelert's grave can be found to this day, near the town named after him, Beddgelert.

But is the story of Gelert true? In Wales, truth can be like the mountains, silent and unmovable. Or it can be like the brooks that trickle through the mountains—ever sparkling, ever changing, ever slipping into time.